THIS BOOK IN YOUR HANDS CAN
ALSO BE HEARD IN YOUR HEAD!

Enjoy your visit.

THE RECOVERY OF CHARLIE PICKLE

A BOOK IN AUDIO AND TEXT

visit eptc.bandcamp.com for "Charlie Pickle" recordings

CONTINUED FROM LAST ISSUE
WITH NINE HOURS HAVING PASSED

8:45 AM.

Northwest Clarence.

THE RECOVERY OF CHARLIE PICKLE, BOOK TWO

Happy Birthday, Susan

WRITTEN AND RECORDED BY ETHAN PERSOFF

Pretty far away from where Charlie lives...

Published by EPTC/HORSE (www.ep.tc/horse) Audio of C.P. was previously serialized on Spoken Word with Electronics. This finished format, audio and text, is © Copyright 2020-2023, Ethan Persoff (Austin TX) Completed text of C.P. Sections 16-22 is assembled here for the first time: October 2023

YOU ARE DRIVING NORTH

An office building can be seen on the right, off of the highway. It has metal numbers on the side of the building, and you see: "9258" in a striking and sculpted Helvetica Bold. Each of those numbers must be 25 feet tall, themselves. The building has no name, only an address: 9258 Highway Road.

The 9258 building is part of a long access road that follows the highway for fifteen miles.

The 9258 building . . .

from its metal numbers
to its guarded lobby
        and its flowers
next to the lobby
viewable from within
the bright windows
outside

. . . is grand in every way.

All the buildings on Highway Road have numbers on them. You can tell the quality of each building depending on how the numbers are presented.

They are either painted on,
sculpted in solid metal like 9258,
or a vinyl decal.

MATERIAL VALUE

One can infer, given that 9258 is a metal sign building, that it might be a better location than 9172, which has vinyl numbers. And all of these vinyl numbers are now cracking and curling from years of sun damage.

The 7 in 9172 is completely gone, leaving behind only a ghost image in the shape of a shadowed out 7 on the building, almost as if a nuclear bomb had gone off, fizzling the 7 onto its facade.

9172 Highway Road was built in the early 1980s. It has all the character of a storage facility. Its entryway is an abrupt elevator, and a stairwell door right next to it. Those are your options walking into building 9172.

The 9172 building is a budget facility for businesses.

There is no lobby.
There are no flowers.
There is no sunlight.
There really are no windows.
There are three ashtrays by the front door.
There are four floors.

And four businesses fill all of its four floors.

Charlie works in office building 9172 on Highway Road.

If the peeling vinyl numbers on the exterior are any indication of neglect due to weather, the same sort of lack of care can be said for its interior, in terms of upkeep.

The building is leased to tenants as
'carpeted with built-in cubicles'.

The brown carpet is torn
in many places and
bumping up in others.

There is a loud buzzing
from the overhead
fluorescent lights.

A drifting, depressive magnetic
field haunts the restrooms.

The cubicles are poorly reinforced and rattle.

If someone working bumps into their cubicle wall,
or even shoves a file drawer with some force,
        you can see it ripple
along
the entire cubicle row,
with
each
paneled
wall:

leaning in
and then
*leaning
back.*   and
       leaning in

   and then

*leaning
back.*
     and then
    leaning in

          and then

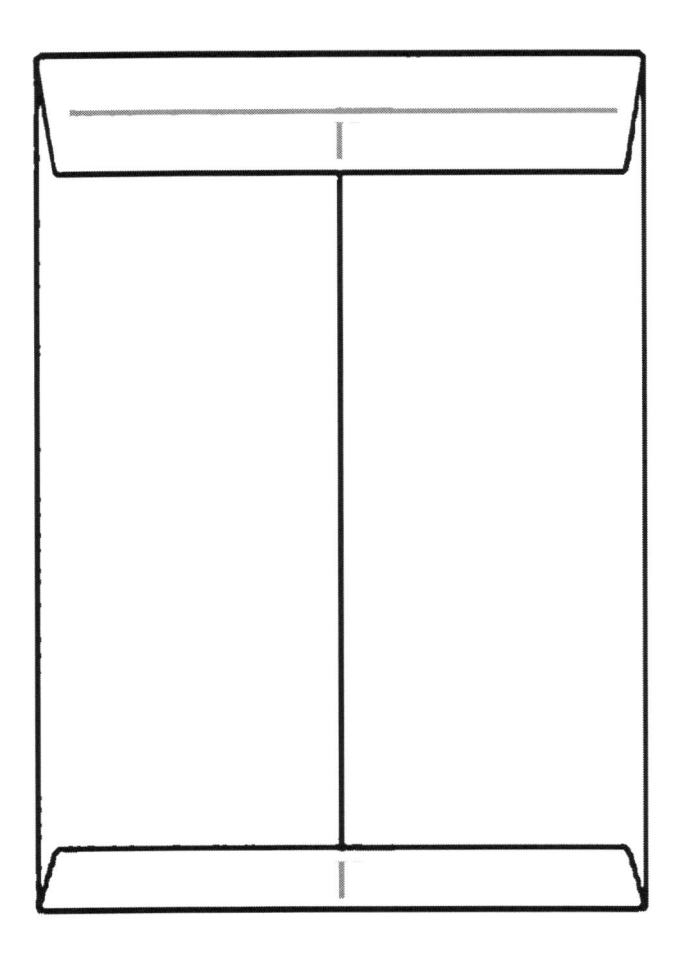

INTER-OFFICE MAIL

Charlie's job is to put numbers in columns, saving this work to a computer file. He then distributes this work to others. These additional workers then add or subtract from his set of data. This work is distributed via printouts and discs, collected in clear tabloid-sized plastic envelopes.

The company has been experimenting with e-mail as a process for sharing this work. But upper-tier management is still skeptical as to how reliable e-mail *is* and are still tied to plastic envelopes for distributing everything that is important.

These spreadsheets are said to be important.

A tap on Charlie's cubicle at 8:52.

It's Brian.

"What's up, Charlie? How's the day today?"

Charlie looks up at Brian and welcomes a few friendly moments of conversation. He'll need to help Brian on some spreadsheets later in the afternoon. But he really would prefer Brian not be around right now.

Each plastic envelope is checked out and accounted for on a clipboard with a sign-in and sign-out sheet. The sheet lists each envelope by numeric order with staging boxes for each check-in and check-out.

All digital work is meant to be saved through a company-issued ZIP disk, which will also go in the envelope. Employees are instructed to print out the spreadsheet and place the ZIP disk in the plastic folder.

Inter-office mail will return the plastic envelope with the ZIP disk, but with the printout removed. A signed sheet indicating the spreadsheet has been received will be inside the plastic envelope. Employees are to remove the ZIP disk and take the plastic envelope over to Karen, who will check it in and stamp the signed sheet.

This is how the work is tracked.

God damnit Brian with the hovering.
Charlie has a few plastic envelopes
God damnit Brian with the hovering.

This is how the work is tracked.

It'd be easier if Brian wasn't here.
God damnit Brian with the hovering.
It should be against the law.

This is how the work is tracked.

Charlie has a few plastic envelopes
to process through before lunch.
It'd be easier if Brian wasn't here.
God damnit, Brian, with the hovering.
It should be against the law
to talk to anyone before 10 AM.

Brian has one more thing to bring up.

"Birthday card for Susan."

Brian hands the card to Charlie.
Charlie looks down at the card.
It is, in fact, a card for Susan,
who is one of the Accountants.

Charlie opens the card to find half of the card filled with signatures and messages. He jokes to himself to write "Fucking Die" on the card, but he restrains himself. He instead quickly dashes out a similar sentiment found on the card of congratulations, and to have a great day, and even adds *an exclamation mark!*, and he hands the card back to Brian. If a nuclear bomb went off at this exact moment, you'd find a shadowcast of Charlie holding out the card to Brian, their silhouettes burned onto the wall for eternity. Archaeologists would try to determine the working relationship between these two mysterious souls. Entire dissertations would be written on the unknown office workers of Clarence, Texas and their curious "greeting card handshake". But no bomb goes off. Brian just smiles and walks down the line of cubicles to get another signature. Charlie begins on another spreadsheet. It's a day like any other day.
Everything feels artificial, as always.

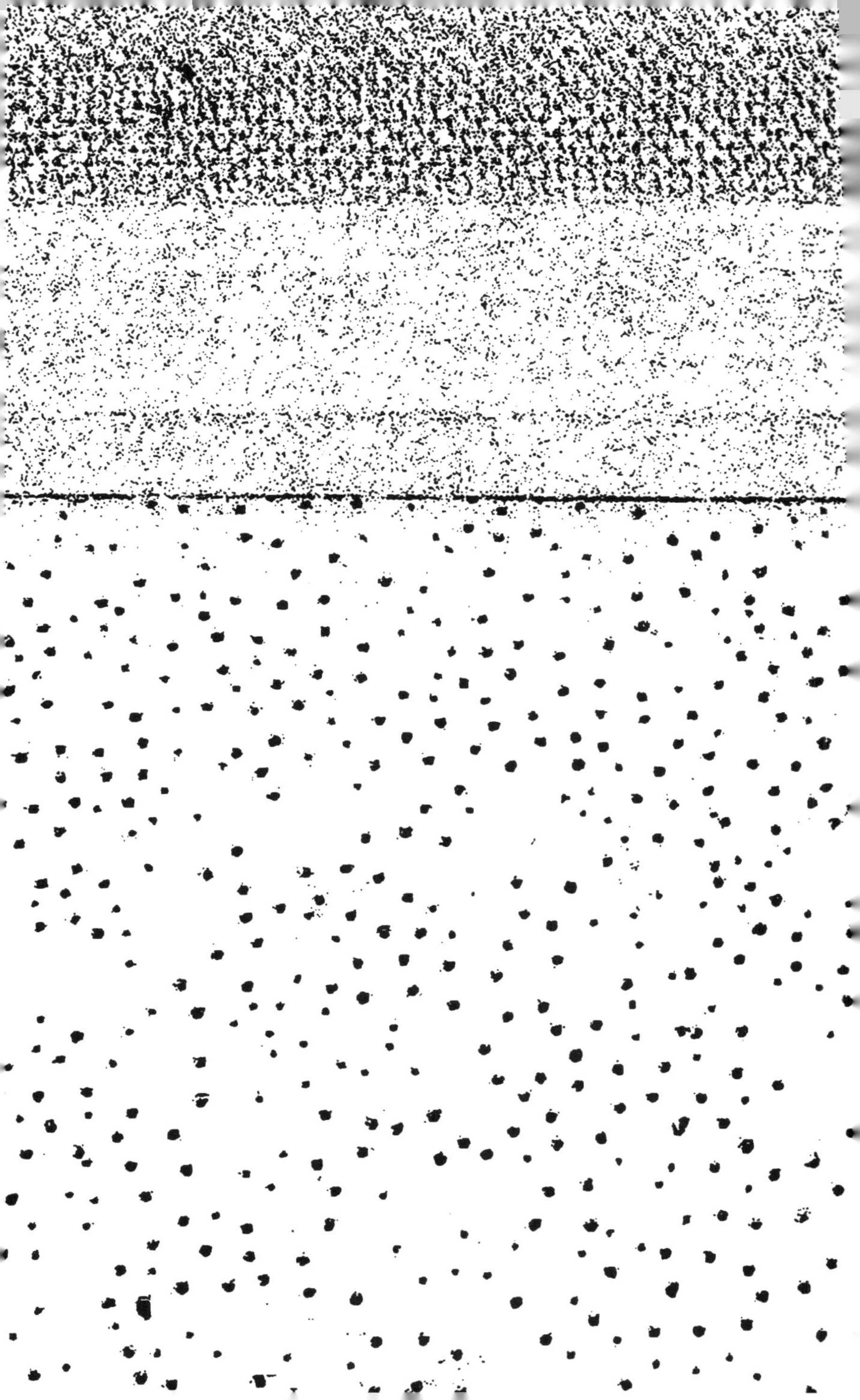

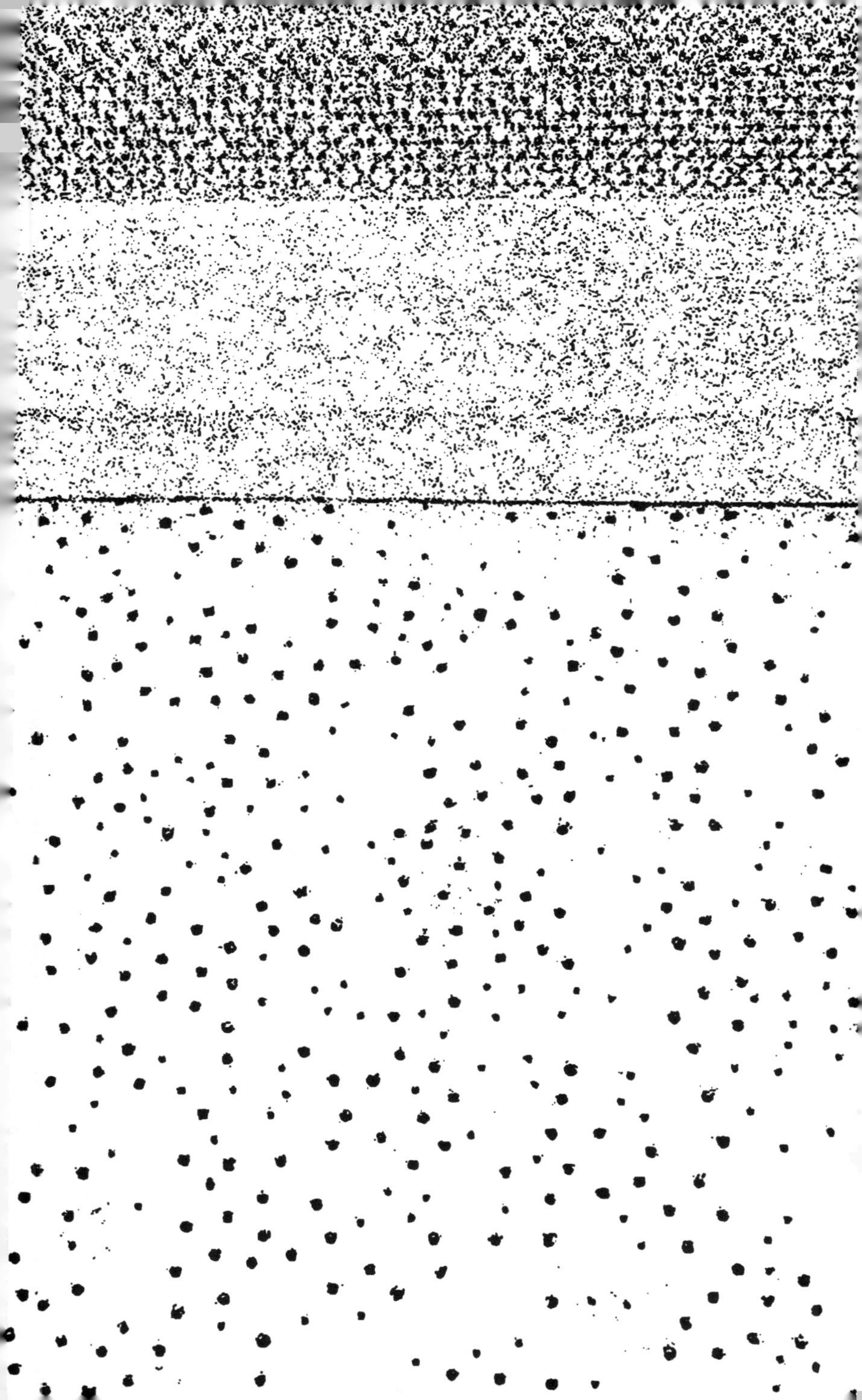

DRINK ALL THE COFFEE

Hi. Welcome to Company Statistics. I hope your first day here is going well. When you're up for it and have a spare fifteen minutes to get away from your desk, please do everyone a favor: Help us drink all the coffee.

You'll find two coffee dispensers in the break room. Go and get yourself some coffee.

The guy before you was a big coffee drinker. We're all a little worried about you filling in where he left off. If you can help us drink all the coffee every day, that'd be a great help. We can give you a Styrofoam cup for today, but for any day after today you're gonna need to bring your own mug. Make it a big mug so you can drink a lot of coffee. The coffee dispensers are a pair of large plastic tubs. Both hold a few gallons of coffee. They each have a pump with a lever, and you press down on the lever to get your coffee. Each dispenser is filled three times a day. Fresh coffee is served at 7:00 AM, at 10:30 AM, and at 1:00 PM. These times never change. This has been a calibrated and time-tested schedule to keep coffee available to employees and to *not waste* any unconsumed coffee. The coffee is poured at near boiling point and cools inside the unheated dispensers to room temperature. In some ways the coffee is too hot when it's first put in there, so I'd wait twenty minutes to get a cup at perfect temperature. But there's gonna be a line at that time. If you wait, you'll have less of a line to deal with, but the coffee will be colder. Remember that the dispensers are unheated. Coffee is a constant discussion when it comes to company expenses. A bulletin to Company Statistics employees states that unconsumed coffee means wasted money. They will know if we don't drink all the coffee.

At each refill, 7:00 AM, 10:30 AM, and 1:00 PM, what is left of the old coffee is dumped into the common sink. And the sink has a draining issue, so coffee poured in the sink remains visible and will not drain. So, to keep the sink clean, all employees are encouraged to consume all the coffee provided or risk having less coffee being prepared.

THE SINK WILL TELL US IF WE ARE MAKING TOO MUCH COFFEE.

Is a handwritten note on the sink.

DO NOT TRY TO DISPOSE OF THE COFFEE IN THE TRASH.

Maybe you like coffee. If that's so, it makes things much more competitive. It's a terrible feeling to encounter an empty dispenser of coffee. But this is all the coffee we have. Sometimes you're gonna find yourself desperately pressing the metal levers on those coffee dispensers to get more coffee from a near-empty jug. But the coffee dispenser *needs* to be emptied, so if somebody's done that to you it's not a slight. Just find your right coffee time every day. We all sort of go at the same times. No one wants any more coffee to show up in the sink is the main point.

When you're in the break room, look at the handwritten labels. There's a story behind that. The labels are masking tape with permanent marker. One label is indicated as COFFEE, ONE BAG the other is stated as COFFEE, TWO BAGS. It makes a pretty strong cup of coffee. And if we want more of it, we have to drink all of it every day.

I guess I'm asking if you like strong coffee. The guy before you did. So I hope you do, too. You have some shoes to fill.

Each hand-written label for COFFEE, ONE BAG or COFFEE, TWO BAGS is a little coffee-stained, torn, and a little brittle. These are just masking tape labels on each decanter, and they've cracked and curled over time. But you'll find the handwriting to be prim and polite.

The person who originally wrote out the coffee labels has retired and died, and there is a Polaroid of her on the refrigerator next to the coffee dispensers. This Polaroid was taken the day the coffee maker was installed in 1987. This was Diane, the previous receptionist. She was a reticent person who was often embarrassed by attention and absolutely hated cameras. She lived alone. In the photo, she's making a rarely displayed "delighted face" as the first coffee is brewed. Diane could have mania, moments that seemed overly-excited and desperate for something to be delighted *by*, only to quickly deflate and become sullen. She was giddy the day the coffee maker was installed. It's the kind of smile that seems unhappy the closer you look at it. But the smile pushes through like a fire drill. It was an unguarded moment for her, not to be recorded, and she was clearly surprised by the photo being taken. An insecure worry is there in the photo with the fear contained in the eyes, aimed antagonistically at the camera as the rest of her betrayed face desperately grins.

"Hey, Diane, SMILE!"

This was said by Bob, with the flash bulb going off like a joke. All of this is caught in the photo. Diane was a very shy person. She didn't have a chance to cover her face or duck away into the sleeve of her blue sweater that she always wore. As the Polaroid developed, Diane saw her face — a full beaming Idiot Grin — slowly emerge, with dazed eyes behind those big, stupid glasses of hers. "Bob, you son of a bitch!", she yelled. — *Quite the reaction from Shy Diane!* — Everyone in the break room laughed. The photo remained there, held on the fridge by a ladybug magnet, where it stayed there for years.

Diane privately despised the photo's existence. She was convinced it was there to make fun of her. But she lacked the fortitude to either remove it or ask for someone else to do the same. For years she was haunted by it, thinking that Bob had placed it on the refrigerator in a shared joke:

DIANE, THE BIG JOKE

Bob always made fun of Diane. Why would he care so much about this photo to display it if it *wasn't* a joke?

Few people understood Diane. And this stupid Polaroid by the goddamn coffee maker plagued her, literally, until her retirement in 1991 and up to 1994 on the day she died.

Diane had always resisted photos, and her family, who had lost even her childhood photos in a fire, sought help from her previous employer for *some* image to be used in her memory. The Polaroid on the refrigerator was all that could be found, and it was used in the funeral program and in the printed newspaper obituary. A miscommunication between the reticent family and the company interpreted that the use of the photo was a loan, however, and it was returned. So there, in the break room today, is Diane's photo. Still on the refrigerator. It just made sense to put it back where it was. Where it originally had been. The ladybug magnet was now holding up some coupons, however. So a Ziggy magnet was used, instead.

Bob is getting old but he's still employed here.

He still says, "Hello" to the Polaroid every day. Even joking, "Hey, Diane, SMILE!!", always laughing. Daily.

You might run into him.

Diane's legacy in the break room is the clear labeling on each of the coffee dispensers. The two bag coffee is meant to be twice as much caffeine, achieved through doubling on the amount of coffee itself. So COFFEE, TWO BAGS or COFFEE, ONE BAG is as much a description for coffee consumers as it is instructions for coffee makers.

There is, of course, next to the two dispensers, the coffee machine which is connected by a snaked plumbing pipe to the wall. You can be burned if you touch it. So building management has covered it in an insulation blanket. The blanket itself has a strong odor from getting wet numerous times over the years. If you follow the pipe to the coffee machine you'll find a button that makes the coffee. Above the button is the plastic container for the coffee grounds. Put one bag of coffee in the plastic bucket, with the coffee filter, for ONE BAG COFFEE, and two bags of coffee in the plastic bucket for TWO BAG COFFEE. You are to press the button once to make a fresh pot. If you press it twice, you will make a mess. This applies to both one bag and two bag amounts. Just one button press for either of them. Both the button to make the coffee and the plastic carriage, to put in the fresh coffee grounds, are covered by a shared wall plate, locked.

Since Diane left, the company has grown to have two receptionists. Both of them have access to the coffee key itself, which operates this wall plate, and also unlocks the coffee drawer. The coffee drawer contains a pre-budgeted set of coffee bags and numerous coffee filters. The office associates trade off the task with a clipboard. Only once in fifteen years of preparing coffee in this manner have they both been out of the office, and on that day there was no coffee. This is because coffee is a perk of the job and not a promise.

The cupboard that holds the many bags of coffee is also below the coffee machine and is locked. Most days find the coffee dispensers less than one-eighth filled at 10 AM.

This is Charlie's favorite time in the day to get his morning cup of coffee. Sure, it might be nicer at 9 AM. Or at 8:30 when he arrives. But the break room is full of people during those times. Nothing is more painful to Charlie than walking into the break room and having to speak with other people. A slightly cold cup of stale 3 hour old coffee at 10 AM is always better, because there's no one to talk with.

He can fill the cup, drink it empty, and then fill a second and make a dessert of the second cup with cream and sugar. This helps get rid of all the coffee, so it's not even selfish. He sits there with his second immediate cup of coffee, neatly finishing off the dispenser until it gurgles a confirming sound of emptiness. He places in a spoonful of powdered creamer and one bag of white sugar into his mug.

He doesn't trust the coffee stirrers. Either the plastic stirrers or sometimes the small wooden ones. So instead he makes his own stirrer by folding the sugar packet into horizontal folds. On the eighth fold, it's as strong as a stick.

Dipping the sugar packet into the cup as a tool, he stirs in the powder.

And in the quiet hum of the
fluorescent bulb above him,

he smiles.

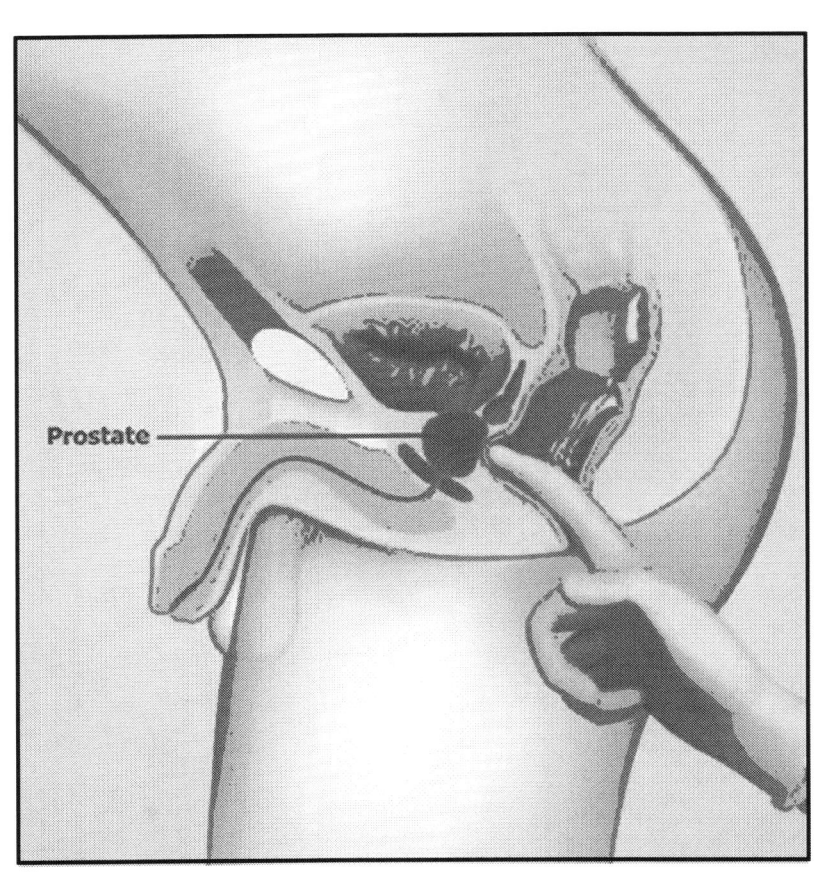

WHITE MAN'S BLUES

WHITE MAN'S BLUES

An empty cup of coffee sits on the desk.

It's around 11 AM.

Charlie has just
completed his
spreadsheet work
for the morning

including a printout
of each sheet on
legal-sized paper

with that printout
set to landscape
for horizontal view

this is to maximize
all the tables
and columns

so that they
can be read on
one single sheet

He packages up the printouts, stapled together in the upper right-hand corner. This is how he's been instructed to do it. Never with more than one steel wire staple. This is to save money. And he transfers these four corresponding files onto a ZIP disk.

Each task is saved as an Excel worksheet file (.XLS) and exported, for redundancy, into a comma separated format, or CSV (e.g. comma, separated, values.) These files have a specific file naming convention, ensuring all project files are grouped commonly together.

The date format is two digits for the year, two digits for the month, and two for the day. Followed by the time in 24-hour format (hour/minute). Followed by a user's unique identifier, which is a five character ID. Followed by the number of the files for that date. So if you're submitting more than one file on a given day, you would numerically ID them as 01 and 02 and 03, etc.

As Charlie has two files to save, he indicates them as REASONER, as that's the account, followed by 981015. That's the date. And PCKLE, for his name. 1105 is for the time of day. And then 01 and 02 for each separate file. Each file is in CSV and in XLS.

It all appears on the ZIP disk as:

REASONER_981015_PCKLE_1105_01.CSV

and then a follow-up file:

REASONER_981015_PCKLE_1105_01.XLS

And then the second file, in identical format:

REASONER_981015_PCKLE_1105_02.CSV

and the follow-up file

REASONER_981015_PCKLE_1105_02.XLS

This is how Charlie spends his day-life at the job.

He drops off the envelope with these printouts and the ZIP disk at the correct location. After evaluation, this envelope will eventually route to Karen, and that will be a different desk. But there is a different person at this desk for envelope pickup on NEW TASKS.

Charlie is now done with his tasks for the week. He's got to pick up a new stack, and Duncan runs the new envelope check-out desk.

Duncan has already prepared the plastic envelope for Charlie. He's included a new ZIP disk inside, and even put in a funny joke, written out in pencil, inside the pack. The note says:

WEIRD HUGS? — ASK FOR CHARLIE!

(Charlie's home phone number is then written out)

"Nice prank, Duncan.
How long has this been on the stack?"

"Hahaha, about a week," Duncan says, chuckling.

This means nearly everyone in the office has had some opportunity to see the message when they've picked up their own envelopes over the last four or five days.

> Duncan shoots a fake gun gesture with his hands, and says, "Pow, Pow! Crossfire!" as Charlie takes his package back to his desk.

> This game, with labels and the envelope, is an ongoing prank fight that Charlie and Duncan have been playing, and Charlie indulges him.

What's offensive, however, is Duncan
has just quoted Stevie Ray Vaughan.

Pow, Pow. Crossfire.

Technically speaking, Duncan is an idiot. This isn't
an insult as much as it's an accurate description.
But Duncan is sweet enough a prankster to charm
Charlie. And they both like to play games.

Outside of work, they'd never be friends. But both help
to pass the time for each other with silly stunts like this.

Duncan is a huge Stevie Ray Vaughan fan. He is
listening to Double Trouble on his Walkman right now.

This music format is what Charlie refers to as
"white man's blues," and he considers it
an exceptionally painful sound.

Clarence has a lot of white men in it.
And white men's blues has a strange cultural
grip on the city of Clarence at this point in time.

If you walk anywhere in town, you will hear it
floating out of cars — like a Caucasian anthem.
The propulsive, empty grunt of white man's blues
is a horrible noise to Charlie.

It's a bit of a perversion of blues, itself.

There are, of course, white men who make blues music.
Townes Van Zandt might be an example that he'd list. But
this silly white man's blues stuff is all action-figure music.
Full of mouth-breathing and odd overbite grinning.

Pow, Pow. Crossfire.

Charlie really dislikes white man's blues.

Duncan, though, as you can already see, is a h-u-g-e fan of the genre. *Especially* Double Trouble. And he has a big permed mullet, which he has grown out in tribute to the format. He oils it all day long, playing with his own curls.

Duncan wears a gold chain connected to a pewter armadillo, which dangles from his neck. And a pewter bat is pinned to his left-side ear.

"Right side's for *GAYS*," Duncan will say; never realizing how many people in the office are privately or discretely gay.

"Duncan, that's a horrible and stupid thing to say," Charlie often points out. Duncan always laughs.

Charlie has half a mind to print out a fake newspaper headline, reporting that left-side earrings now indicate a homosexual preference. But he avoids it, as that would be outside of the rules of their prank fight. Because Duncan might believe it and become terrified.

Duncan is a nice person, after all, just a genuine idiot.

If you catch Duncan on the street, you will find him in a cheap Stetson hat with a feather in it, and a brown leather duster jacket — just like his God.

This has been Duncan's style for ten years, since he adopted it in 1988. *(RIP SRV!)* When asked if he'll ever stop wearing this clown suit, Duncan likes to say:

"When the King returns from his premature death!"

Then hollering:

"Come-ON! Can't you see, I'm strand-ded!"

He would then go off into an air guitar riff of Stevie Ray Vaughan's Crossfire.

So it's best to just tolerate the music heard from Duncan's headphones and not ask him anything about it. Pretty much any question about Stevie Ray Vaughan will result in Duncan screaming Crossfire at you.

Pow, Pow.

Charlie pulls out a notepad and begins to write out on a stationary to-do list:

"Reminder: Murder Duncan and crush his tape player"

He thinks to place the note in his newly available plastic envelope, wondering how many other desks in the office it would pass over before circulating back to Duncan.

Pow, Pow.

Pretty much everyone shares the same perspective on the shrieking, desperately hormonal guitar sounds. Two can play the same game, Charlie jokes, finishing off the Murder Duncan note, and sliding it into the sleeve.

ELSEWHERE . . .

on a helipad about five miles away,
is a 58 year old man named Morton.

He is also a fan of Stevie Ray Vaughan.

And he is loudly playing the same terrible music.

He shares the same heterosexual-sided earlobe preference as Duncan. But instead of a pewter bat, he has upgraded to a single pearl earring.

And unlike Duncan's stupid kindness, a sort that might accidentally misspeak, Morton's anger at the world is much more attuned towards hating people intentionally.

"Fags" is his chosen epithet for gays, along with worse terms for browns or blacks. Which is ironic, considering his love for the blues. Some of the best blues singers were gay black singers with brown lovers.

But this is white man's blues he loves.

"...Let's do this for Stevie," he says.
"...Let's do this for Stevie."

He keeps on saying this to himself, clicking switches on, as the helicopter, which he's rented for the hour, hums to life. A very expensive hour, at that, and paid in full.

Morton takes Stevie Ray Vaughan even more seriously than Duncan, including Vaughan's death by helicopter. It's something Morton takes to be a spiritual message. Morton is in trouble with the I.R.S., and he'd like to send his own message today.

MORTON'S LAW

Never call Morton 'Mort' for short.
Or heaven forbid ever calling him
'Mott' by accident.

"Are you calling me a damn Hoople?,"
he'd say, revealing his age.

Morton is a person who finds offense at simple things.

Like mispronounced names!

Red lights at traffic intersections!

Or other barriers in his right of way.

He finds great anger, in particular,
in transactions of m-o-n-e-y . . .

like delivery fees, service fees,
or fixed tips!

. . . that are beyond his control.

"Everyone's in it for just a little bit more than they deserve!" is something Morton used to yell at his wife. This was before his wife left him for infidelity. And then his mistress left him for a sudden lack of cash.

He hadn't filed taxes for fifteen years, and the I.R.S. had just seized his business assets. And on top of that, they'd fined him an additional $200,000.00.

> This all gave Morton
> a tremendous amount
> of white man's blues.

    and he played his   Double
                                            Trouble
                                            as loud
                                            as he could!

During an audit, you could hear music in the background of taped conversations.

Morton is angered when he is asked to turn the music down.

It's at this point in the recording that Morton screams about:

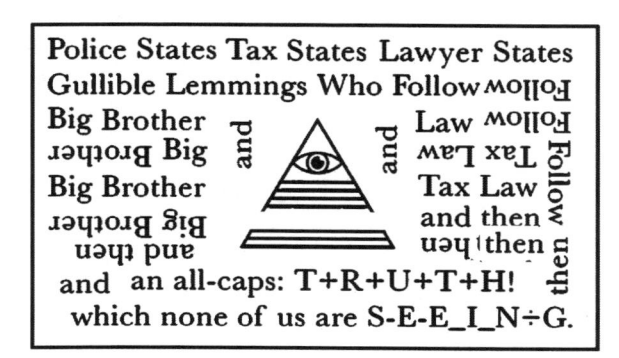

> Police States Tax States Lawyer States
> Gullible Lemmings Who Follow Follow
> Big Brother and △ and Law Follow
> Big Brother and ▲ and Tax Law Follow
> Big Brother   Tax Law Follow
> and then   and then then
> and an all-caps: T+R+U+T+H!
> which none of us are S-E-E_I_N÷G.

And if we could just fucking L÷I÷S/T/E/N . . . he'd tell us all about it. But we'd be too stupid to understand, he'd say, cranking up the Double Trouble.

When Morton lost all his assets, he claimed in court that taxation was against his rights as an American citizen.

The judge mentioned that he sounded very Patriotic, to which Morton smacked his fist in agreement.

"You're damn right."

"How do you think America pays for its upkeep?" the judge asked.

"In particular, I believe that some paved roads might have been needed to have been made to deliver those audio cassettes to you, sir."

The judge was joking.

THAT FUCKING JUDGE!

Morton had been listening to Double Trouble on low volume to help get him through the trial. He'd claimed originally that the ear piece was a hearing aid. For one very yellow moment, Morton was shocked to be found out — listening to Stevie Ray to get through the trial.

His memory of the court case is a distorted view where the entire room began laughing at him. The laughter has only gotten louder in his memory as he replays both the court trial and his meeting with I.R.S. personnel in his head nightly.

The I.R.S. and the judge are presently
a mob of hippos in his mind.
Hungry, hungry hippos!
And those hippos are gonna burn.

Morton had used the last of his remaining savings for helicopter lessons and to secure a private helicopter license. The final amount of his money would be spent on this one hour rental of the helicopter, along with insurance fees from the helicopter school itself.

His instructor, incidentally, cannot stand Morton.

The instructor considers Morton to be seemingly annoyed with everything. Morton is especially furious about the Government for his tax issue.

Morton has a lot of white man's blues about those taxes.

He double checks the gallon jugs of extra gasoline behind his seat. And right around before noon, he lifts up into the air.

"Let's do this for Stevie,"
he keeps on saying to himself.

Pow, Pow. Crossfire.
Pow, Pow. Crossfire.
Pow, Pow . . .

Northwest Clarence is the cultural desert of the city. It is predominantly tar and asphalt. Very few trees. A shallow creek bed has dwindled to a mere puddle in Northwest Clarence. This creek once flourished deep in the heart of town, but the constant concrete inlays of Northwest Clarence constructions stopped much of the water from being absorbed into this part of the city. So the more business that gets built in Northwest Clarence, by way of office buildings or other development, the drier this part of town becomes.

Charlie leaves the 9172 building, off Highway Road, and passes underneath the highway, itself.

He hears the traffic above him as the concrete of the overpass bounces from every passing car.

He walks uphill to a small row of businesses. These are just some small shops, assembled to serve the employees of the highway buildings. He grabs a sandwich at the franchise sandwich shop, which is about two blocks away.

In the landscape of various buildings along Highway Road, there is one shiny one with metal letters on its facade.

This is the I.R.S. building, and it's easy to spot.

9258 Highway Road is less than a mile away from Charlie's place of business at 9172, but 9258 is visible for miles due to its veneer of better building materials, which are shiny, particularly its metal Helvetica lettering. The lack of tree cover in Northwest Clarence makes it all the more visible.

The ostentatious and flambuoyant appearance of the 9258 building makes it hard to miss in the air as a target. And it's as Charlie orders a sandwich, a rented helicopter smashes into the window of 9258 Highway Road, exploding.

The rectangle block of metal numbers on 9258 is one of the first things hit by the chopper blades of the helicopter, as it folds and crumbles in midair into the main corner of the structure, shattering and erupting into fire.

The I.R.S. has a strict rule about early lunches. It bans them, particularly structuring when meal times can occur. And those rules do not permit a lunch break until 12:15. It's 12:05 presently.

Many workers inside are killed instantly and even more are trapped inside and injured. A few people at ground level are bleeding from fallen debris.

Alarms all over the city sound off.

Unaware of any of this, Charlie calmly eats his lunch, which is a toasted roast beef and mayonnaise.

With yellow peppers.

>   And tomatoes.

A BUS WILL BE HERE SOON

It's the smoke detectors that first alert authorities that the 9258 building has been attacked. Though it will be some time before the term ATTACKED is used in any official description of events. The alarm's log report will first merely indicate a FIRE on the top floor. Once it is determined that a helicopter has hit the building, the word ACCIDENT is then presumed. At that point, officials begin using the word ACCIDENT as the cause. It's an *alarming* circumstance, but remains a standard 911 call at this point. A series of fire trucks immediately respond, along with medical and police.

But the fire is so intense inside the top floor of the 9258 building . . . and the view of the helicopter is said to have been so horrifying in its straightforward approach that surviving witnesses, along with people who viewed it from across the street in adjoining buildings, cannot help but scream about this being deliberate. There was something far too intentional about the helicopter slamming into the I.R.S. building. They all say:

"It is an ATTACK!"

And, as Charlie continues through his sandwich, such person-to-person hysteria is building, growing in loudness, as phonecalls motivate other phonecalls, and local talk/news radio picks up on the dog whistle.

"Citizens of Clarence, we are under ATTACK!"

"Americans, we are under ATTACK!"

"This was NOT an ACCIDENT!"

By this point, it has been twenty minutes since 9258 has been hit by a helicopter.

The local radio stirs it up:

"Why hasn't the city said anything? Are we presently at WAR?!"

No one will know for a while that this is the result of a single person's protest. Either direction this story takes, it will certainly be the lead on the news for tonight and the next three or four days. National attention is even likely. And regardless of intent, many people in 9258 are dead or injured. Gasoline is in the air. This is a lousy afternoon.

Charlie finds himself less concerned than others.

Presently, he is oblivious to what is happening outside. His only worry is lunch and finishing it in a satisfying and good way. The sandwich he ordered seems to be dry.

He returns to the front counter to get some relish or a workable condiment. He opts for a spontaneous bag of chips, plucking a bag from a nearby basket.

He walks up to the register with two bucks. "It's only 85 cents for the bag of chips," the cashier says. Charlie grabs the top cup off the stack of waxed cups, and says, "Yeah the rest is for some iced tea."

The employee says, "All right, cool. This will do it." And he hands fifteen cents to Charlie. Charlie says to keep the change, as a small tip, appreciating the kindness of the moment. The gesture is worth more than the dime and the nickel. They both smile at each other and Charlie moves on to get his unsweetened iced tea from the iced tea dispenser. Charlie skips over the bucket of lemon wedges and avoids adding any sugar. It's the caffeine he wants. He takes an immediate sip. "Mmmm! This is very good iced tea," he says to employee, adding, as his head zips up, "A lot of caffeine in this!"

The employee nods, wiping down the counter.

"It's always good to take an early lunch," Charlie notes, overcome by the boost. "You avoid the crowd!"

ARE THERE NOT LAWS AGAINST HELICOPTER-SLAMMINGS?

Outside, ambulances and police cars buzz by quickly.

The sandwich shop is a franchise, but it inherited a building with no windows. This building was originally a bar, and a very discreet dark bar. So now it is a dark bar turned into a dark sandwich shop.

Charlie walks with his tray and his completed sandwich on a paper plate. He puts everything in the trashcan and tells the person behind the counter to have a good day. The door dings as Charlie leaves.

Somehow the sound outside has waited until that moment to fly into the space. The eyes of the sandwich shop employee grow wide. He leaves the counter and runs over to the closing door, yanking it back open to peer out. He sees Charlie walking away in a kind of confusion, but the employee then loses Charlie in the crowd. It's all so much to hear and see.

BUSINESS DISTRICT IN CHAOS

The street is one giant cluster of noise. People are running around and going out of their mind. It's as if a bomb has gone off. And literally, be it the hysteria from the radio or the helicopter hitting the building, something explosive *has* just happened. As people run by, the nervous sandwich shop employee quickly shuts and locks the door. He slaps the CLOSED sign on the window. The indoor sign spins around on its string, vibrating lightly from the outdoor foot traffic.

EVERYTHING IS LOUD

Atmospherically, it's the smoke that Charlie first notices. And then it is the screaming — the sounds of an array of urgent yelling around him. Everyone wants to be away from this part of town. Alarms and honking. Cars are screeching and colliding, continuing on, not even stopping.

Charlie stops to observe one of these collisions and a woman slams into his shoulder, not even looking back, running far across the road. A car slams its brakes to avoid hitting her. It squeals its tires to resume its previous speed. Everyone wants to be away from this part of town. They will all calm down once they've gotten away from the Highway Road district. But they have to get away from it first.

Charlie looks up into the air and sees police helicopters and news helicopters. Suddenly, military jets appear, making a grid of white smoke on a perfect light blue. The long lines of smoke resemble sidewalks.

He has to calm himself during this moment.

Charlie looks up and thinks of walking on one of those sidewalks up in the sky. How much quieter it would be.

He wonders if he'd be walking on the sidewalk with his head facing down towards the earth, or on the other side of the sidewalk, with his head facing up to the sky. Thinking about this calms him a little bit more, as more people run past him and other people scream and other cars honk, peel out, or collide with one another.

But this thought experiment on
the jet stream sidewalks isn't working.

As everyone around him is going wildly out of their minds, Charlie stumbles forward. He knows what's going to happen. The trigger always appears first on his forehead, with a specific thin line of sweat. This is followed then by a pinch in his left sinus. He knows that he's having a very sudden, very specific panic attack. And a very familiar one. He's about to pass out.

He sees a beacon of hope in the alleyway. There's a bag of garbage. It's just soft enough to catch his fall. He gets there just in time. He slams onto the alley ground and everything gets suddenly much louder and then dissipates in the hues of color and rubber-like sound.

Then it all quickly
mutes

        into a dark

                unconsciousness.

HEY KIDS! CATCH THE NEW SHOW! "HOW MANY FACES" 6 A.M. MONDAY – FRIDAY ! SPOT ALL THE FACES. DIFFERENT OPTO-CASES EVERY TIME! SOME HAVE MANY FACES. SOME HAVE NONE! DO YOU SEE SEE THE FACE(S). "HOW MANY FACES", weekday MORNINGS

call in & win prizes

DO YOU SEE MY FACE? OR DO I NOT HAVE A FACE?

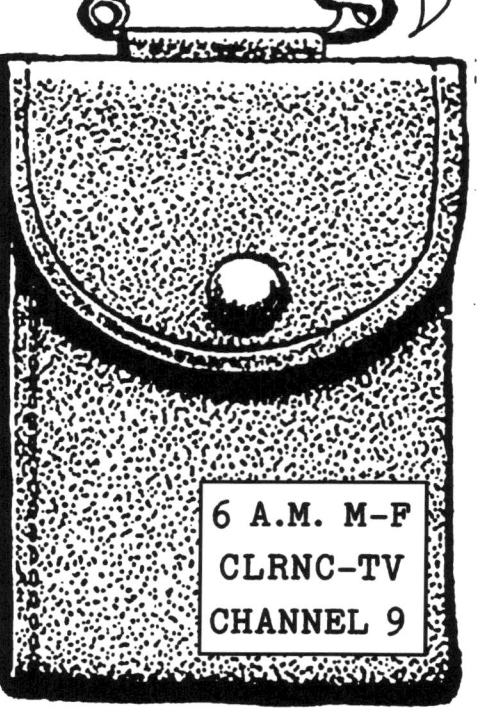

6 A.M. M-F
CLRNC-TV
CHANNEL 9

THE VOICE OF CLARENCE
CLRNC-TV CHANNEL ⑨

HOW MANY FACES

A SENSE OF TIME HAVING PASSED

A light, quiet breeze. Charlie opens his eyes.

A dried leaf is kicking around in the air, near his forehead, It goes skipping around in the alley. His nose then awakens to the plastic damp bag of trash that is his pillow.

He quickly remembers, "Oh, it's been another one."

> He used to get these a lot, especially during high school. Now he gets one or two a year.

He realizes he's had another collapse.

Many times this has resolved with Charlie waking up from these in a hospital bed, though once he was taken to the drunk tank at the police station. A few times he woke up in a stranger's home. Many times he wakes up with a missing wallet. People stole from him even when he was nine. He's always wished that other people would ignore him when he passes out. He thought about getting a card made asking such neglect to take place, but he didn't want to encourage himself by making that card, as that would seem to accept these attacks are part of who he *is*. But today, however, he seems to have received his wish. Unmolested. It's likely nobody even saw him fall. And if they did, they just ran right beyond him. He wakes up where he fell. There's garbage on his face. This is lucky garbage, because it caught most of him in the fall. There is no concussion, no sprained jaw, no chipped tooth. It was a perfect landing.

Looking up at the skies, it seem to be about 4 PM. That

would be about four to five hours that he's been out. He's surprised at the duration. It's perhaps a personal record.

"I guess it was that kind of a moment," he says to himself. Charlie gets on his feet. His back and his legs hurt a bit, but it must have been a clean fall. The lack of machine noise is very peculiar. This is a business district and the street right now is completely empty. For rush hour on Highway Road, it is ominously quiet.

He thinks to ask the new shift at the sandwich store about what's going on, but he sees that it is closed and its door is locked. The sky is gray and he hears nothing from the highway.

That's an amazing sound: Nothing from the highway.

And then his sense of authority, or fear of it, jumps into play, and he says to himself, "Good grief, I am late to work!"

Charlie starts panicking anew.

He needs to call.
He can't find a payphone.

He begins quickly walking back to his building. He takes the same path he took to get a sandwich, but in reverse. He's walking fast enough to nearly be running.

Charlie walks down a hill and
approaches the highway underpass.

This will lead to his office.

Walking under the overpass feels wonderfully dissociative. It is normally filled with bouncing cement blocks from the constanly ricocheting car traffic above. But to Charlie's bemusement, there is only complete emptiness.

Walking out of the overpass, to his right, is the highway exit. There is normally a row of cars in the process of leaving the highway, either stopping at the light or racing the light and buzzing ahead. But nothing. No cars.

Charlie can't help but consider walking up this empty ramp and standing on the highway itself. To be in the oncoming, but now empty, way of traffic. And before he realizes it, he is right there, completely forgetting about returning to work, standing in the center lane.

An empty highway at the peak of what is normally the beginning of evening rush hour. It's a Thursday. Probably about 4:30 at this point. He touches the concrete . . . He even lays down. He doesn't want to ever forget this moment. And then, getting back on his feet, he walks back down the ramp, back down the highway exit. He aims himself at building 9172. It's just a short walk away.

Normally the 9172 office building has a sense of activity when you near it. Even though you can't see in, when you approach the building you get a sense of something happening inside. But approaching the 9172 building today, it seems almost dead. It's this point in the horror movie where someone might scream, "Where is everybody!"

But Charlie walks to it unfazed. He's not complaining. This is actually incredibly beautiful and very comforting. This is somewhat of a fantasy come true for Charlie.

Especially if a bomb actually did go off . . . and Charlie is the only human left on the planet. Oh my god, how great. But he has to confirm this. He stands in front of his building and pulls at the door. It is locked. He pulls again.

It is then that he hears the voice.

" HANDS UP ! RIGHT NOW . "

Charlie is pale with fear. It's the kind of voice that can only be attached to a gun. He's heard it before. This is a police officer's voice. Charlie does exactly what he's told.

" KEEP THEM UP ."

Four officers run up to Charlie, pulling him back into their grip. Two of them run their gloves up and down his body, squeezing his legs, pinching his armpits, and wrestling his hair. His entire abdomen is padded and pressed. A shuffling sound of heavy fabric and metal.

Charlie feels the beginning of a line of sweat on his forehead. He hopes he won't be passing out. But fortunately, his other instinct takes over. He will be compliant and cool.

He thinks to himself, "Be compliant and cool."

Compliant and Cool.

He is handcuffed.

He tries to think about something other than what is happening. He needs to forget about their guns. He focuses instead on the weight of their handcuffs.

> "My, these handcuffs are heavier than I would have expected," he says to himself.

Charlie focuses on the weight of the heavy cold steel surrounding his wrists. "These likely weigh as much as a pound apiece," he thinks. And he stays under control.

Everything is going to be fine. Compliant and Cool.

Charlie's wallet was fortunately not stolen from him when he was unconscious, so it is there to be found by an officer during the pat-down. The wallet is yanked out of his pants and handed to another officer. Charlie is spun around. He is still held at his shoulders. His neck is starting to hurt by the way he is being handled.

The officer receiving the wallet is the one who had first addressed Charlie at the doorway. He keeps his gun trained as he looks through the billfold. Inside he finds Charlie's company I.D. and his drivers license.

The officer calls both pieces of identification in. The officer turns back to Charlie.

" THIS IS A CONTROLLED AREA. HOW DID YOU GET HERE ? "

Charlie is Compliant and Cool.

"I went out for lunch some hours ago . . . Officer, I have a medical issue where I pass out . . . That happened to me today. There was some hysteria outside . . . I passed out. I just woke up in an alley, up the road. I work in this office building and I'm just trying to get back to work."

And then to Charlie's humiliation,
he apologizes:

"I'm sorry."

" WE ARE DEALING WITH A PUBLIC SAFETY ISSUE. THIS ENTIRE THREE-MILE SECTION IS CLOSED OFF TO THE PUBLIC. DID YOU NOT THINK ANYTHING ABOUT THAT WITH THE *LACK OF CARS* ? "

Charlie doesn't want to escalate this, so he states to the cop, "I want to be helpful. What is the best way for me to answer you and be helpful?"

(THE COPS ARE SILENT)

"Please, I do not want this to escalate . . . I'm just as surprised as you . . . "

(THE COPS ARE SILENT)

". . . I just woke up, and no one was here."

This attempt at reason and honesty frustrates all of the police officers, especially the commanding one. Something very bad is about to happen. But a callback then comes over the radio, confirming Charlie's identity. He does in fact belong here.

He needs to legally be allowed to leave.

Charlie is then led into a police car, still in handcuffs, and driven to a bus stop, five miles out. The door is opened, and Charlie's handcuffs are removed.

Charlie is handed back his wallet.

" STAY AT THIS STOP . DO NOT MOVE . WHEN A BUS ARRIVES , YOU ARE TO BOARD IT . "

Charlie looks up at the bus sign
and sees that it's a Number 12.

"I don't know how to get anywhere
from this route," he says to the cops.

" WHILE YOU FIGURE THAT OUT, MAYBE ALSO THINK ABOUT HOW LUCKY YOU ARE THAT YOU ARE NOT DEAD ! "

The police are furious at Charlie. They
clearly wanted this to go differently.

"Thank you, Officers . . . I will."

Compliant and Cool.

"I am sorry I was there."

Compliant and Cool.

"I appreciate your work for the city."

Smile. Take their bullshit. Survive. The police car revs its engine and zooms back to its previous location, likely repeating this process with anyone who walks into the closed off three mile perimeter.

"Police safety issue, my ass," Charlie thinks,
"these cops are having the time of their life."

Charlie can still smell smoke in the air. Something must have happened, but he still has no idea what. He looks up at the bus sign and sees that it's at least a southbound route . . . This will get him aimed in the right direction, at least. So he calms down from the near-death event of having a gun aimed at his head.

Charlie sits down on the bus bench at the bus stop.

"A bus has to show up here eventually,"
he says to himself.

Charlie had taken the bus this morning, in fact. It would have been very helpful if the cops had dropped him off at a familiar stop. That would have been any Number 3.

But this route is unfamiliar. It's a Number 12.

Still, "a bus will definitely be here soon," he says.

His legs are shaking.

He's sitting down on the bench.

This is where they dropped him off.

This is where they want him to be.

Get home and figure out what's happening later.

Just survive this weird moment.

Compliant and Cool. Survive, Survive.

A bus will definitely be here soon.

HURRICANES AND DISPLACEMENT

In 1968, a large hurricane threatened much of the Gulf, and numerous cities were marked as sanctuaries for any displaced people near the Texas coast.

The largely emptied buildings of Clarence would house beds for the poor from all over the State.

This was of course during a celebrated year for drug use, and as the hurricane drifted away from Texas, Clarence kept its new citizens, reemerging for a summer as an open-air party for drugs — particularly pot and a new recreational brain toy, called Acid.

The air of Clarence was delighted by its new population.

There was little to no police presence remaining, the bank having repossessed the station, and no taxes to pay for civic protection. Much of Clarence, for one or two beautiful summers, became a haven for the truly demented, young, and insane.

Nudity became commonplace, and a small commune was established outside the town, where they began growing tomatoes in the mud. They moved into the emptied storefronts, bringing a changed narrative to the entire location.

Eventually, these hippies, or peaceniks, or monsters, animals, or whatever you wanted to call them, became their own citizens of the city. They began to take on their own possessions. The electrical grid and other city services never really went anywhere, and the population was allowed to grow back on its own new trajectory.

The son of the mayor publicly promised to not arrest pot smokers — and was elected sheriff. A new city council even got a Chevy dealership to move in.

Soon it was 1970, and Clarence was getting back on track. A new factory had moved into town that packages Saltine crackers. The radio P.S.A. said it all:

Clarence is on its way back!

And if you were one of those Hippies that moved into Clarence in the late 1960s only to become a normal person working at either the Saltine factory or the movie theater or one of the new bookstores or the diner, you might have at one point saved the money to get yourself a new or used Chevy, and you might drive south of the city one beautiful night towards the Treemont Reserve. You might want to test your engine and go mudding along the backroads — alongside Treemont — following its barbed wire fence for miles, up and down the inclines of the private land. At one point, you might encounter some cement and some tar.

If you're high enough, you might think to yourself:

"Nature is so random, it can even grow a road."

It would become clear in the moonlight, that there's a wild road right outside that beautiful garden of trees.

The road makes little sense, aimed nowhere, but maybe some other roads will join it later. You'll have to tell others about it, even though they won't believe you.

That single road is, of course, Sunset Drive.

Two main roads would eventually overlap onto Sunset in 1971, making it a small, imperfect, unplanned detour.

SUNSET DRIVE

was sold to a small home builder, and as per the agreement, the small profit from its sale went 51% to the Treemonts, and 49% to the 100 seated investors, though finding all of the individual investors across the country would prove a challenge.

SEVEN SMALL HOMES

would be built in 1972. All these homes were designed to be used as rentals. Most of these homes were created to be duplexes. And by 1998, the year in which you are presently in, the seven homes of Sunset Drive have not aged
badly at all.

THE #12 ROUTE ARRIVES

(HOME AND SAFE SOON)

The southbound Number 12 Bus,
after about 45 minutes of waiting,
    suddenly appeared
        in front of Charlie.

  He saw it edge over the hill
    and approach him.

  Getting larger
    and larger
        as it got nearer
        and nearer.

  And with a great breath of relief,
  Charlie got on the Number 12.

  "Does this connect anywhere
  with the Number 3?"
  he asked, paying his fare.

  "Yeah," answered the driver,
  "There's a Control Depot.
  Six or seven routes all hit that.
    Number 3'll be there.
    We stop there, also."

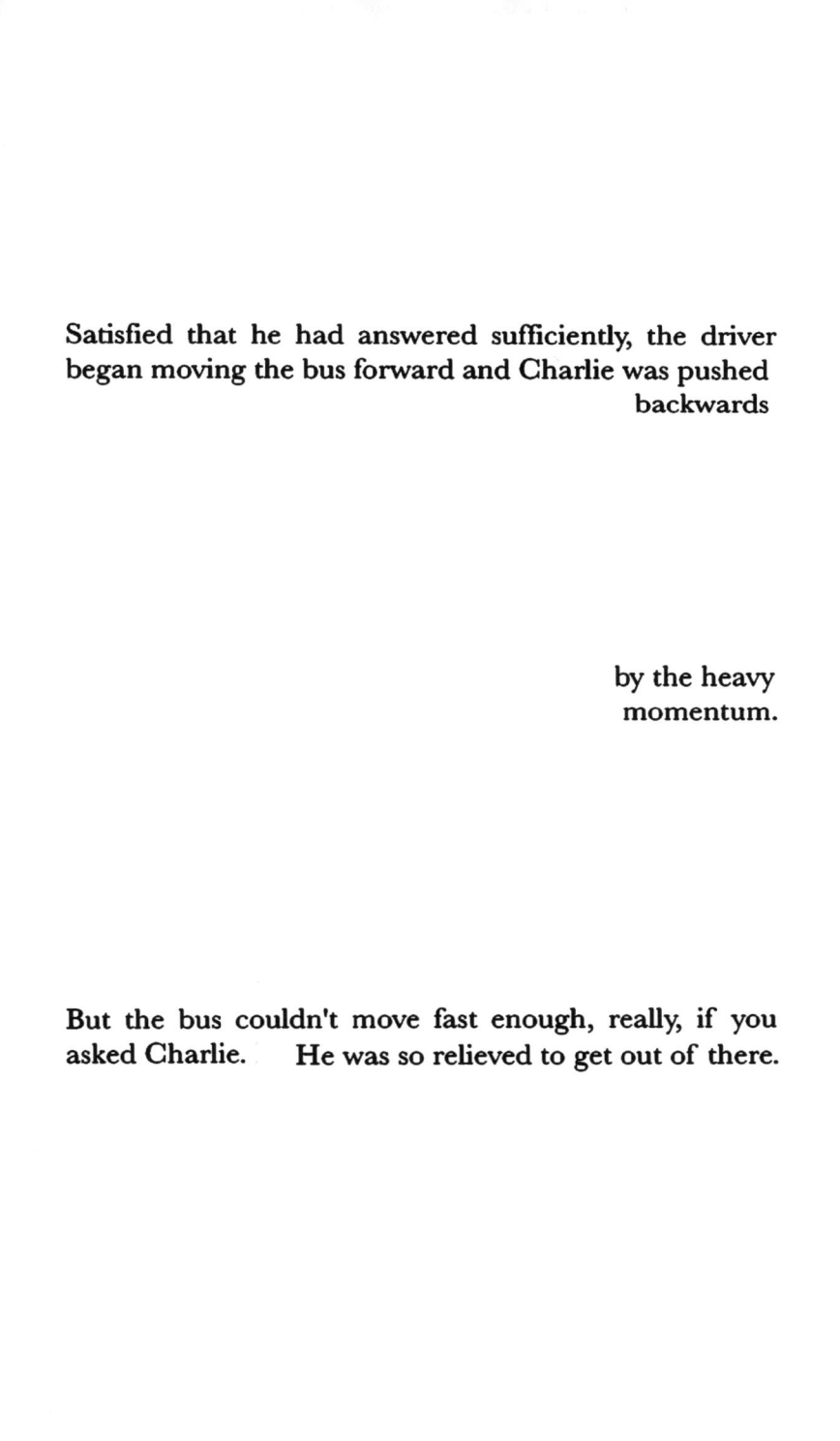

Satisfied that he had answered sufficiently, the driver began moving the bus forward and Charlie was pushed backwards

by the heavy momentum.

But the bus couldn't move fast enough, really, if you asked Charlie.   He was so relieved to get out of there.

ROUTE CHANGE

The bus began a detour around downtown, which had been announced. But many hadn't been listening. As the bus veered off its normal course, a group started yelling:

"BUS DRIVER, STOP!"

"DRIVER STOP! YOU'LL MISS MY SPOT!"

The source of the detour, a helicopter hitting the I.R.S. building, was still publicly considered an accident.

A few riders didn't think it was unintentional, though. So Charlie heard talk bordering on all sorts of conspiracy.

"It just couldn't have been an accident"
"Fucking I.R.S. had it comin' to 'em"

Talk like that.

It would take the Number 12 a couple of hours to get to the connecting Depot that the driver described, and Charlie caught the very last Number 3 going South at that time at about 1 AM.

When he got on the Number 3 there were about four other people. Three were just drunk or tired, bobbing their heads, and the fourth was an older woman who seemed to be returning from work, probably from a grocery store or something.

And then for the final fifteen minutes of his trip,
he was the only one in the bus.

They went over a bump

and the lights on the bus went completely out
and Charlie was the happiest he'd been all day,

the only rider on a bus that
was completely pitch black,
going South, towards home.

The bus driver didn't even
ask him how he was doing.

Then there was no conversation.

That bus ride could have
taken three or four hours

and it wouldn't

have bothered

      Charlie.

He was very happy.

He'd soon be home and safe.

He'd be home and safe soon.

Some time around 2 AM,
the Number 3 bus drops Charlie off.

He's very familiar with this stop.
It's is at the bottom of a hill,
and Charlie will walk up that hill
back to his home on Sunset.

He does so in the silence of the moonlight.

Very still street.

Remarkably empty of cars.

Charlie walks down his alley, and he
enters his home via the backyard.

He returns to find a light that he'd left on inside the garage this morning. This seems like days ago, and certainly not the same 24-hour period. So many things have happened. But he shuts off the light and returns to his proper space inside.

The home is as he left it, still in some disarray
from the unexplainable disruptions of the night prior.
But it now feels solidly empty and solidly welcoming.

The home is happy to see Charlie and wonders where he's been and why he is returning from work so late.

"Why Charlie, it's nearly 3 AM," the house observes.

It will be a full hour until Charlie's thoughts are able to shut down. Then he normally can sleep in until 8. At that point, he has to wake up for work. A quick five minute shower and he'll be out the door by 8:15.

So getting to bed, he thinks it's gonna be okay.
>Make some use of his Friday.
>>Perhaps RESET the incredible
>>activity that went on today.
>>>Transform it into a NORMAL FRIDAY
>>>end-of-week day of work.

Charlie's spinning mind
finally quiets down at 4:15.

>And he

>>drifts
>>into a

>>>>deep   sleep.

EMPLOYEE CHECK-IN

An hour before the 8AM wake up, at 7, Charlie is raised from the dead in a panic. his phone screams out, urgently ringing.

"CHARLIE! — "   He picks up.

"CHARLIE. I'VE BEEN TRYING TO GET AHOLD OF YOU ALL NIGHT. WHERE HAVE YOU BEEN?"

> It's his boss, Harland.

Charlie looks down to his digital answering machine. A red display blinks **09** above a label for **MESSAGES**.

"Sorry . . ." Charlie says. "I'm just now seeing all these calls.   . . . What's up."

"WHAT'S *UP*? ARE YOU A FUCKING IDIOT? I ALWAYS TOOK YOU TO BE A SMART ONE, PICKLE. WHAT'S *UP* IS THE WHOLE BUSINESS DISTRICT WAS ATTACKED YESTERDAY IS 'WHAT'S UP'. — JESUS, ARE YOU THAT DAFT!"

"Oh, so it WAS attacked?, I..."

"THE I.R.S. BUILDING WAS, YES. MY GUESS. WHAT IT MEANS FOR US IS THE I.R.S. IS NOW OUT OF A BUILDING, AND THEY'RE MOVING INTO OUR BUILDING, STARTING TODAY."

There's silence on Charlie's side of the phone.

"ARE YOU DEAF OR MUTE? LISTEN! I JUST TOLD YOU THE I.R.S. IS NOW WITHOUT A BUILDING. SO THEY ARE MOVING INTO OUR BUILDING. AND WE ARE BEING FORCED TO MOVE OUT. — CAN YOU AT LEAST JUST GIVE ME A FUCKING PULSE OVER THE PHONE, PICKLE!"

Charlie starts laughing. "Excuse me," Charlie says, reexamining the blinking number nine on his machine.

"So now you've called me ten times to mention this?"

"YES, TEN TIMES IF YOU COUNT THIS ONE, AND NINE BEFORE IT. YOU'RE A FUCKING MATH WIZARD. THE REASON IS: YOU ARE OUT OF A PLACE TO WORK. DO YOU UNDERSTAND? WE ARE *ALL* OUT OF A PLACE TO WORK. CHARLIE. — PICKLE. — MISTER. — PICKLE. LOOK AROUND. . . . ARE YOU AT HOME?"

"Yes, you're calling my home phone number. I'm at home."

HOME
"WELL, WELCOME TO YOUR NEW OFFICE! WE'RE GONNA TRY THIS NEW IDEA CALLED TELEPHONE COMMUTING!"

"Okay. . . . So I still have a job."

"OF COURSE YOU STILL HAVE A JOB. AND OF COURSE I'M STILL YOUR FUCKING BOSS! GOOD GOD! - I THOUGHT YOU WERE A SMART ONE, PICKLE."

"Okay."

"OKAY. SO THIS IS BASICALLY IT: I'M GOING TO CALL YOU BACK WHEN YOU NORMALLY CLOCK IN. THAT'S 8:45. CORRECT??"

"Well, Harland, I show up at 8:45. But that's some wiggle room to start at 9 ..."

"WELL, YOU'RE NOT GONNA *BE* FUCKING COMMUTING BY FOOT OR CAR TODAY, SO I THINK YOU'RE STARTING AT 8:45, RIGHT?? I'M SAVING YOU SOME DAMN TIME, RIGHT??!"

"Right."

"OKAY. . . . WAIT FOR A CONFERENCE CALL AT 8:45. IF YOU ARE NOT THERE TO PICK UP THE PHONE AT 8:45, I WILL CONSIDER YOU LATE, PICKLE. GOT IT!"

"Yes. . . . Got it."

Harland's phone then slams down on the other side of the line, with an audible clang of plastic and a bell before disconnecting with a striking click. Charlie listens to the dial tone for a full minute. He needs to hear the comforting off-hook signal to calm himself. And he continues to stay on the phone until it goes silent.

Charlie makes a mental note to not forget the call at 8:45.

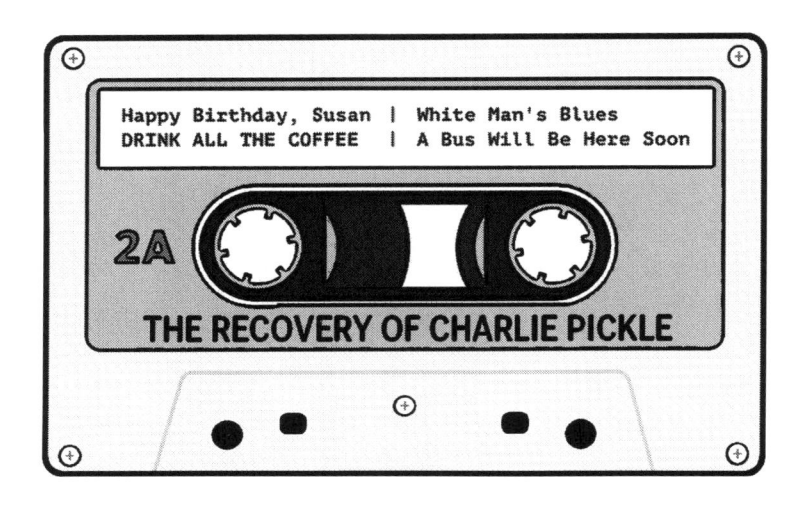

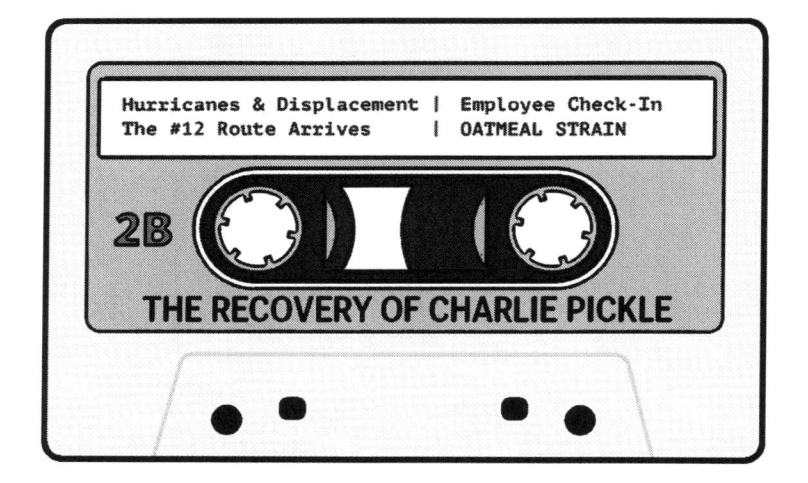

2A — THE RECOVERY OF CHARLIE PICKLE
- Happy Birthday, Susan
- DRINK ALL THE COFFEE
- White Man's Blues
- A Bus Will Be Here Soon

2B — THE RECOVERY OF CHARLIE PICKLE
- Hurricanes & Displacement
- The #12 Route Arrives
- Employee Check-In
- OATMEAL STRAIN

eptc.bandcamp.com

OATMEAL STRAIN

(The Arrival of Harland Atwater)

"...Well, that phone call went perfect."

Charlie's boss puts down the phone and stares for a moment at his kitchen wallpaper.

>The wallpaper is a green and white pattern of flowers with orange details and black lines for the petals.

>The kitchen still has a lingering smell of bacon from breakfast, and two bowls of oatmeal lay in the sink.

He looks at the sink for a moment as his wife Barbara walks into view.

"Barbara . . . Looks like you missed some of the oatmeal on the rinse."

"Harland. It doesn't matter."

His wife grabs the oatmeal bowls and rinses them, spitefully replying, "If you remember, we're using better soap now. The dishwasher takes care of it."

"Well, Barbara. No telling how much the life of the dishwasher is affected by us not doing our part with the rinsing. Do we want us to kill the machine over OATMEAL STRAIN?" Harland replies.

"Oatmeal Strain?" Barbara asks. She's immediately annoyed.

"Yes. The extra exerted effort of the machinery . . . The strain against the gears . . . To clean the dried oatmeal off the bowl!"

Barbara wants to ask Harland if there's a section on *Oatmeal Strain* in the Operations Manual for the dishwasher. Or if he has any idea how a dishwasher works. He's certainly never operated theirs. She'd also like to ask him why he can't clean the dried oatmeal off his bowl himself as hers was perfectly clean, and he's bitching at her about his own bowl of oatmeal.

But these conversations have happened before, and the ending of these conversations - with amplified new corrections from Harland is never worth the effort.

Instead, Barbara rolls her eyes.

She scrubs the plastic oatmeal bowl to a shine, shaking it in the air, and with some frustration, she places both oatmeal bowls on the top rack of the dishwasher. She then looks at the clock.

"You're late, Harland."

"Not today, love," Harland answers. "Do you remember the magazine article I was reading last month about the mobile jobs?"

Barbara shuts the dishwasher with a click, answering, "vaguely . . . the one about the telephone employees?"

She'd love this conversation to be over and have Harland out the door for the day.

"Telephone Commuters!" Harland answers.

"The shorthand for that is tele-commuting, Barbara."

Barbara examines something behind the toaster.

"And let me tell you, Barb. Bob was gonna pay everyone to just stay at home while this I.R.S. building issue is figured out."

"Right . . ." answered Barbara, suddenly realizing Harland might not be leaving for the day.

She presses the toaster back against the wall.

"Well, I, instead, said, *'that is ridiculous'*, and everyone else seemed to really appreciate me pointing that out. *'Pay people to just stay at home?'* I said. Everyone really thought I was onto a roll, there. *'What a waste of money and time!'* I suggested. Man, Bob looked like an idiot."

Barbara looks around the living room for a reason to leave the kitchen and get out of this conversation. She finds the newspaper on the coffee table and moves to pick the paper up and refold it.

"So what are you saying, Harland? Are you at home today, then? Are they paying you to be at home?"

"No, do I look like a waster? Not at all. It's much better than that. I got the Administration Office to approve my idea about tele-commuting, Barbara. And our team will be still working, but they will be *at home.* If it's successful, and how can it not be, then *everyone's* gonna try my tele-commuting idea. This is a big moment, Barb."

Barbara has already turned on the TV in the living room. "Well okay, Harland."

She has little idea what he's referring to, but has a very sad, sudden feeling that he's clearly going to be around today.

She switches channels to her morning game shows.

Satisfied, Harland walks outside to have a cigarette.

This might be the beginning of a great new role for him at Company Statistics. Their top guy in an emerging field. Tele-Communications Manager. He can just see it, engraved in beveled white on a black plastic plate:

Harland Atwater
TELE-COMMU!-BOSS!

"Success is only found through opportunity"

Harland says to himself.

He then looks at the neighboring row of homes and begins to assess each home for individual flaws and infractions . . .

1   That red car looks like it is parked crooked. He also doesn't recognize it.

2   Someone else seems to have left on their front door light from the previous night. That is just going to invite a burglar.

3   A few other homes have not picked up their newspapers.

4   And it looks like the newspaper boy himself has been throwing the paper irregularly!

An unnatural pattern
        of newspapers line up crookedly
                up and down the block.

Suddenly, a nice DING goes off in his head:

The paint on the home, two doors down, is looking slightly dry and *cracking*. Probably needs to be repainted . . . Bingo. He'll have his opportunity to contact the H.O.A. about possibly issuing a note!

Just then he looks at his neighbor, Ted.

Ted is outside, hurriedly getting into his car.

"Ted, a bit late today, I'm seein!"

"Fuck off Harland," Ted thinks to himself, instead politely replying:

"Thanks, Harland. Quite the Clock Watcher!"

"Motherfucker, Harland," Ted grumbles to himself, once inside the security of his car.

He turns the key on his ignition, and as he backs up out of his drive, he sees Harland smoking from his front door, still assessing Ted with his eyes.

Ted thinks of pressing his breaks, changing the gears forward, and then pounding the gas, slamming into Harland — in such a way that Harland would explode blood and bones right there. Like a popped blood vessel on his front door. But he worries Harland would just correct him about doing it incorrectly.

Instead, Ted continues backing up, and watches Harland evaluate the speed and angle of Ted's exit.

After completing a survey of the street for all other possible errors, Harland finishes his cigarette, which he properly disposes in a flower pot.

This is designated by Barbara for his cigarette butts.

Happy Barb, Happy Harl.

He goes inside.

Today is an exciting day for the future manager of tele-communications.

He checks his watch.

He has a conference call to make . . . in 22 minutes.

END OF BOOK TWO

ALSO AVAILABLE
FROM EPTC/HORSE

THE BUREAU
Back in print. A comic book with a nine hour story, which is meant to accompany nine hours of your life. A timestamped panel for every track. Book and 200-track Album available. Electronic music with decisions.

RECOVERY OF CHARLIE PICKLE BOOK ONE
Read the first issue of this ongoing story. Meet Charlie, who is asleep. Look around at the woodwork. Is that maple moulding? Some carpet wouldn't be bad in the hallway. Life and death answered. Book and Album available.

JOHN WILCOCK, NEW YORK YEARS
Want uncommon history? The story behind the creation of The Village Voice, The East Village Other, The Underground Press Syndicate and much more. Ten year undertaking. LARGE BOOK. "A deftly presented Bio-Comic that illuminates New York's mid-century Underground Press Movement" — The Washington Post

For information on all titles
see us at http://ep.tc/horse

Made in the USA
Columbia, SC
10 November 2023